Double Cross

DONOVAN BIXLEY

upstart press

In memory of Joe Cool, a hound with lots of battle scars.

 Disclaimer: The publishers advise not to let your pets perform deadly stunts on the top of trains.

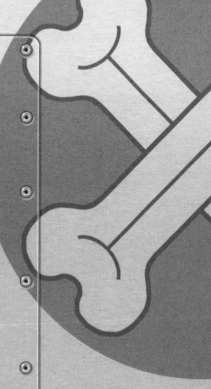

A catalogue record for this book is available from the
National Library of New Zealand

ISBN 978-1-988516-17-2

An Upstart Press Book
Published in 2019 by Upstart Press Ltd
Level 4, 15 Huron St, Takapuna
Auckland, New Zealand

Text and illustrations © Donovan Bixley 2019
The moral rights of the author have been asserted.

Printed by 1010 Printing International Limited, China

MEET SOME OF THE CHARACTERS AT CATs HQ

Claude D'Bonair's mother was a dancer and singer in a Paris nightclub who fell in love with a dashing stunt pilot from America. She worries that Claude is too much like his daredevil father — who went missing in the Himalayas during one of his great adventures.

Syd Fishus has a lot of guts. He can handle any dangerous mission and still have plenty of guts left for slow-cooked lobsters and cream. He once sailed across the Pacific with Claude's father, and developed a taste for coconut crabs.

Commander Katerina Snookums wants to win the war so that cats and dogs can live together in peace once more.

General Fluffington has a wicked sweet tooth — he even likes sugar on his jellymeat.

Major Ginger Tom is the most famous dogfighter in all of katdom. He is heir to the Earl of Cheshire and distantly related to the Queen.

Yuki is the owner of Le Chat Blanc Café, in Paris, but this mysterious feline is also one of CATs' top spies.

Mrs Cushion likes doing crossword puzzles. She is the General's tea lady. She knows just the way he likes his tea *and* all his other secrets.

MEET SOME
OF THE DOGZ

Alf Alpha is the leader of the DOGZ army. He believes that only pure-bred dogs should rule the world. His loyal troops call him 'The Furrer' and he gets very *short*-tempered if anyone mentions his size.

The Red Setter is the DOGZ' top fighter ace and gets his nickname from the unmistakable red Fokker triplane he flies. The Red Setter descends from a noble dog family and his favourite things are poetry, dancing and flying.

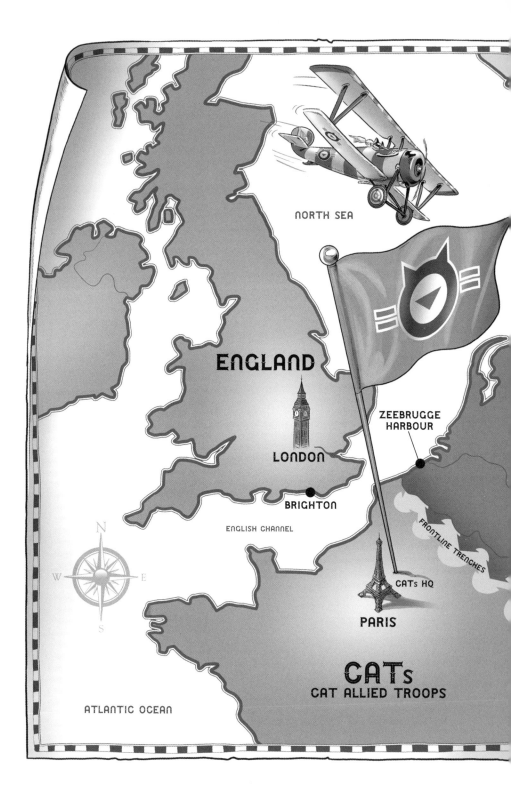

DOGZ
DOG OBEDIENCE
GOVERNED ZONE

BERLIN

EUROPE 1917

The great war continues. Cats and dogs once lived together in peace. That was before a pack calling themselves DOGZ took over the kingdoms of Central Europe. As the invading DOGZ army conquers more countries, the Cat Allied Troops (CATs) have gathered from every corner of the katdom to save Europe from going to the DOGZ.

CHAPTER

'**S**izzling squid suckers!' shouted a street seller.
'You've already eaten,' said Claude D'Bonair,
hauling his friend Syd Fishus away from the food
stalls at London's East End markets.

The two pilots from Cat Allied Troops, or CATs
as they were known, had been sent for a spot of rest
and relaxation in England's capital city. Even on
holiday there were plenty of reminders that CATs
were at war with the DOGZ army. Claude gave a
worried look to the horizon, where barrage balloons
dotted the skyline. From these hot-air blimps hung
wire-cable nets. Enemy planes would be caught like
flies in a spider's web if they attacked the city.

'Relax, mate,' grinned Syd. 'Let's enjoy our reward
for saving CATs' chief inventor on our last mission.
The war isn't coming on holiday with us.'

'But spies from the DOGZ army are sure to be
on our tails,' said Claude. 'Their leader, Alf Alpha,

will be out for revenge after we destroyed his gigantic flea bomb in Egypt.' Claude pointed to a newspaper. 'Just look at these headlines!'

NEWS STAND

THE MIDDAY SUN

DOUBLE-CROSSING SPIES IN LONDON.

The Red Setter swears he doesn't dye his fur.

'Crikey dingo,' snorted Syd. 'Only mad dogs and Englishmen read *The Midday Sun*. Look mate, the English Channel is between here and the DOGZ army. Who would be spying on us?'

Claude tried to relax, but his cat senses were prickling – and in fact, nearby someone *was* watching the two pilots very carefully.

'We're on holiday,' continued Syd. 'What could possibly happen to us in magnificent London? No secret missions, no dangerous battles, no death-defying rescues. There's only one thing we have to save . . .'

'What's that?' asked Claude.

'We have to save room in our tummies for all this food.' Syd followed his nose to a stallholder who was calling out to passing cats.

'Use ya watch and chain guv. Wrap ya laffing gear 'round this Isle of Skye for ya Tommy tucker.'

Syd nudged Claude. 'Is he speaking English?'

'It's Cockney rhyming slang,' Claude explained. '"Watch and chain" is your brain, "laffing gear" is your mouth, "Isle of Skye" means pie, and "Tommy tucker" is supper.'

Syd licked his lips. 'I like the sound of Isle of Skye for my Tommy tucker.'

'We've only just had lunch,' Claude reminded him.

'But I'm still a bit peckish,' said Syd, eyeing up a blackbird pie.

Claude sighed. Only Syd could still have an appetite after all the feasting they'd done on their holiday. In only a few short days they'd been from one end of London to the other, travelling on the city's famous red double-decker buses.

Top Tourist Sights

 Visit Queen Vic-Clawria's crown jewels and see the royal orb, designed to look like a ball of string, topped with the world's largest diamond.

Join hundreds of tourists chasing the pigeons at Nelson's scratching post in Trafalgar Square.

Climb Big Ben clock tower, for wonderful views of the the city.

 Go inside the dome of St Paw's Cathedral.

 Shop at Harrods, the famous department store where you can buy anything from the cat's pyjamas to a fine-toothed flea comb.

Head out of the city to historic Bonehenge — where ancient Bone Age druids performed their rituals, thousands of years before the cats' conquest of 1066.

 See the giant doodle of a dog carved into the chalk hillside on Salisbury Plain.

'You already had kippers and cream,' Claude was saying, reminding Syd of the lunch they'd eaten at Harrods. 'And that was only your side dish! Syd?'

Claude glanced back and forth, but Syd was nowhere to be seen. Claude heard Syd's voice coming from a side alley. 'I know I shouldn't be doing this, but no one at CATs needs to know.'

'It will be our little secret,' said another voice.

'That's the plan, mate,' said Syd.

Claude headed down the alleyway and bumped into Syd coming out of a darkened doorway.

'What is *that*?' said Claude, eyeing a package of large triangular biscuits in Syd's paws. 'Are those . . . *dog* biscuits?'

'I got hooked on them after our mission to Switzerland,' confessed Syd, with a guilty look on his face.

'Where did you . . . ? Never mind, you can throw them in the rubbish.'

'The rubbish!' cried Syd.

Claude looked about nervously. 'With all this news of DOGZ spies in London, we can't take any chances with dog biscuits. If someone was watching us, they might think *we* were double-crossing spies.'

'But they're delicious dipped in chocolate,' moaned Syd, inhaling the freshly baked smell. 'Nobody's going to arrest us for eating dog biscuits!'

At that moment a car with blacked-out windows roared up beside them. Two cats in military uniform leapt out.

Syd quickly hid the biscuits . . . in his mouth.

'What are you doing?' demanded one of the soldiers.

'Ugh gagga wabba ba,' said Syd, through a mouthful of crumbs.

'We . . . we're not doing anything,' stammered Claude. 'What's this about?'

'You've been under surveillance,' said the soldier. 'We've been ordered to bring you in.' He nodded to his partner. 'Sergeant Pepper, put them in the car.'

'Yes sir,' she said, and ushered Claude and Syd into the back seat. The doors slammed shut. With a screech of tyres, the car with the blacked-out windows sped away.

VAROOO

CHAPTER 2

The black car raced through London's streets.

'Where are you taking us?' said Syd angrily.
'It's not illegal to eat dog biscuits! You can't prove a
thing. I'm Captain Sydney Fishus of CATs Air Corps.'

'You betta calm down,' said the officer who was
driving. 'I've got orders to bring you in, and
no one said I 'ad to be nice about it.'

The car took Claude and Syd across
the River Thames and into the heart of
the city. Unlike the East End markets,
this part of London was all grand stone
buildings and old palaces.

The car turned off the main street and headed down a side lane, where it came to a halt outside an optometrist's.

Sergeant Pepper escorted Claude and Syd inside.

It seemed like the shop hadn't served any customers since the war began. Behind the counter was an old cat, with a face that looked like he'd run into a locked cat door.

'Pussycat pussycat, where have you been?' growled the flat-faced cat.

'I've been to London to visit the Queen,' replied Sergeant Pepper.

'Right you are. That's today's password,' said flat-face. He pressed a button.

On the back wall, a full-length mirror tilted, revealing an opening. Claude and Syd were taken through a secret passage that resembled a carnival house of mirrors. Their reflections surrounded them like an army of crazy clones marching off to infinity. The Sergeant ran her paw down one of the mirrors and it opened into a whole new world.

'This is CATs Eyes,' said Sergeant Pepper.
'The control centre for our worldwide intelligence
network.' Everywhere, cats were busy decoding
messages, plotting troop movements, and listening in
on DOGZ radio communications.

The Sergeant herded Claude and Syd into a lift which took them to the top floor. There were more desks and tall windows giving them a spectacular view of the city.

London's skyline stretched from St Paw's and Tower Bridge all the way to Westminster Palace. Directly outside was Big Ben clock tower. Two great barrage balloons hovered in the sky above, protecting London's most famous landmark.

'I don't know why they bother with those ugly blimps,' said Syd. 'The DOGZ have given up dropping flea bombs from hot airships, and a DOGZ fighter plane would run out of fuel long

before it reached London.'

The Sergeant took them down a corridor with offices for CATs' top commanders, including Admiral 'Eyepatch' Jellicoe, head of the CATs navy, and Field Marshal Monty Muffin of the army. The Sergeant knocked on the last door.

'Enter,' came a voice.

Inside, a small feline was staring out the window with her back to them. She turned around.

'Commander Snookums!' exclaimed Claude, relieved to see his commanding officer from CATs HQ in Paris.

'Sorry for all the secrecy,' said Commander Snookums. 'Thank you Sergeant Pepper for bringing these two in.'

'Marm,' nodded the Sergeant, shutting the door as she left.

'If this is about dog biscuits,' said Syd. 'I can explain—'

'Captain Sydney Fishus, not everything in life is about biscuits.'

'So I see!' puffed Syd, eyeing a packet of cat biscuits on Commander Snookums' desk.

'For your information, this package contains secret intelligence,' explained Commander Snookums. She gave Syd's wandering paw a slap. 'It comes from one of our spies, a New Zealand cat who is so tiny we call her "The White Mouse". She helps cats escape DOGZ territory and gets them to our friends in The White Paw.'

The White Paw were rebel dogs who had turned tail to fight alongside Cat Allied Troops.

'I'd still be trapped behind enemy lines if it wasn't for The White Paw,' said Claude, remembering the time he'd been shot down in a dastardly DOGZ ambush. 'So how does this biscuit message work?'

Commander Snookums continued. 'To the average DOGZ soldier, this package seems like an everyday product.

NANNA MUNCHKIN'S CAT BISCUITS

'We use a special code to decrypt these symbols on the label. They tell us the location to meet our secret agents. The number of biscuits inside the package tells us what hour of day the meeting will take place.'

'Ingenious,' said Claude. 'And to think we were just here for a holiday.'

'I didn't bring you to London for a *holiday*,' said Commander Snookums. 'I've brought you in for an urgent reason.' The Commander offered them a seat.

'Claude, your mission to Italy brought us the plans for a brilliant new fighter plane. Unfortunately, the designs are like a jigsaw puzzle, and we are missing the key piece that will join all the parts together. If we can get this piece of the puzzle, we can put this fighter plane into our battle squadrons and bring an end to the war once and for all. Your mission is to safely bring this last piece of the puzzle back to our airbase here in London.'

'It'll be a piece of cake,' said Syd. 'After our holiday we're fully loaded and ready to roll.'

'Hmmm,' muttered Commander Snookums. It certainly appeared that Syd's stomach was fully loaded, and quite capable of rolling as well.

Commander Snookums leaned close. 'We know that the DOGZ have a spy within CATs HQ,' she whispered. 'I don't know who I can trust. That's why I've called you both in. I can't tell you any more here. Be at King's Cross train station this evening and await my instructions.'

Just at that moment General Fluffington bustled into the office. The General's tea lady, Mrs Cushion, followed close behind. Syd's mouth fell open when he saw her trolley wobbling with delicious jellies.

'Shivering shih tzus!' boomed the General. 'Roll your tongue back in, Syd. We're civilised cats, not blathering bloodhounds. Now off you go.'

As the door closed behind them, Claude and Syd heard General Fluffington say, 'This is more like it. A top-secret meeting with extra jelly on the side . . . and don't forget some biscuits with my tea, Mrs Cushion.'

General Fluffington slurped his tea. 'Are you sure we can trust those two?' he asked, after Claude and Syd had left. 'The DOGZ spy is someone close to one of our top commanders. We need a loyal cat who follows orders.'

'Claude D'Bonair is no lapdog,' said Commander Snookums. 'He's proved himself time and again. He's just the type of hero we need to whip these DOGZ. I would trust Claude with my life.'

Meanwhile, Mrs Cushion continued to pour the tea looking a lot more interested than she should have done.

CHAPTER 3

Street lamps glowed like little yellow moons as Claude and Syd made their way to King's Cross train station. All the walking made Syd look like a steam train, with little clouds of breath puffing out of his mouth. Every so often Claude was sure he could hear the click of boot heels following them, but when he stopped, the footsteps stopped too. Perhaps it was just his own footsteps echoing.

King's Cross was packed with soldiers lugging their kit bags as they boarded the trains that would take them to the coast. Boats would ship the soldiers across the English Channel and then on to the front lines in France. Families crowded the platforms hugging their loved ones, and soldiers hung out of the carriage windows for their last goodbyes.

Claude and Syd stood nearby, disguised as everyday cats.

'Want a spit and polish?' came a voice.

'Excuse me?' said Claude, looking down.

'Spit and polish ya boots, guv,' said a tiny wee kitten holding a shoe-shine kit.

Claude crouched down and jangled a handful of coins from his jacket. 'You shouldn't be working the streets,' he frowned. 'Have you had something to eat?'

The shoe shiner flashed a grin and pocketed the money. 'Commander Snookums said you were kind,' she laughed.

Claude was astounded. This little poppet was one of Commander Snookums' spies?

She opened her shoe-shine kit and handed the contents to Claude. It was a packet of cat biscuits with a design printed on the label.

'This is a code for where and when to meet our next contact,' Claude told Syd. When the two pilots looked up again, the little shoe shiner had vanished into the busy crowd.

'Quite the undercover agent!' marvelled Claude.

The bag contained cat biscuits as well as train tickets under false names. Claude passed one to Syd.

SOUTHERN RAILWAY
1 X 1ST CLASS CABIN TICKET FOR
Mr F. Boomsticks
overnight train
DEPARTS: King's Cross Station, London
082

SOUTHERN RAILWAY
1 X 1ST CLASS CABIN TICKET FOR
Mr S. Kinny
overnight train
DEPARTS: King's Cross Station, London
081

'I can't be Mr F. Boomsticks,' Syd complained.

'They're just fake names,' said Claude. 'What difference does it make?'

'It doesn't suit the character I'm developing,' said Syd. 'Know wot I'm sayin', eee right bye gum old chap.'

'What *are* you saying?' asked Claude.

'I'm torkin' English I is. So we can blend in right good, diddly old sport.'

'Fine,' laughed Claude. 'I'll be Mr F. Boomsticks. I know you've always wanted to be S. Kinny.'

'Hey!' said Syd. 'You should have seen me in my swimsuit when I was a kit. I was a late bloomer. Everyone used to call me skinny-dip.'

'I can picture the dip but not the skinny,' sniggered Claude. 'Maybe you should drop the accent though. If we're going to retrieve the secret puzzle piece we don't want to draw any attention to ourselves.'

As Claude and Syd boarded the train, a figure was watching them from the shadows.

Far from King's Cross station, on the other side of the English Channel, there was a DOGZ submarine base in the Belgian harbour of Zeebrugge. Showers of sparks lit up the night as workers put the final touches on a very special submarine.

Watching over the scene was the DOGZ' most famous fighter ace, The Red Setter.

ALL HEEL
ALF ALPHA

A soldier scurried up and saluted, before handing over a note. The Red Setter read the message and smiled. *Excellent*, he thought, *our spy in London has made contact*. The Red Setter had an important mission and it was time to launch. Those CATs would leap out of their fur when they discovered what was coming.

The train carrying Claude and Syd clickety-clacked
as it chuttered through the English night. It passed
through sleepy towns with quirky names like Little
Netherwhiffing, Bitton by Fleah and Widdle Upon
Shrubsbury. Every so often the steam whistle
would toot as they zoomed through a tunnel. Then
the train would clickety-clack on, past hedgerows
standing to attention in the moonlight.

   'So where are we heading?' asked Syd. He and
Claude were sitting in the train's dining carriage.

Claude was working out the code on
Commander Snookums' message.

'We're headed south to the sunny seaside,' said
Claude. 'These symbols read "Brighton Pier".

'Let's head back to our cabin. We'll check that packet of biscuits to find out what time we meet.'

They squeezed down the corridor, past soldiers and nurses heading for a midnight snack in the dining carriage. Syd groaned and clutched his round belly.

'Are you feeling okay?' asked Claude.

'I ahh . . . well, Nurse Mitzi said I should start counting what I eat,' said Syd. 'I think it's a terrible idea. Even thinking about it gives me a tummy ache.'

'I'm proud of you,' said Claude, as they approached their cabin. 'It'll be great for your health to eat less.'

'Yeah, about that . . .' began Syd, but Claude suddenly held up a paw, stopping Syd in his tracks.

'Look!' said Claude. 'The lock on our door has been broken.'

The two pilots burst into their small cabin. There was a roar of dark wind. Papers flew everywhere.

Claude flicked on the light just in time to see a figure disappearing out of their cabin window and

into the night. The intruder was clutching the bag of
cat biscuits!

Claude had been trained in the martial art of
Meow-zaki, and he leapt after the thief.

Claude spun around to see the gaping mouth of a tunnel racing up to engulf him. He dived flat. The top of the tunnel sliced overhead.

Claude was smothered by a choking cloud of blackness. All he could do was cling on, with his eyes and mouth shut against the burning smoke. He was almost out of breath when the train finally gave another toot. When the carriage burst into the clear night Claude was grasping an empty coat. The thief had got away.

'They vanished into the night,' Claude told Syd, back in their cabin. 'It would be impossible to search the entire train with all these soldiers on board. It could be anyone.'

'It was a DOGZ spy for sure,' said Syd. 'They turned our room upside down looking for clues.'

'They must have been following us since London,' sighed Claude. 'Now they have our secret message. They'll know exactly what time to meet our contact.'

'Actually they won't,' confessed Syd.

'What do you mean?'

'You know how I was counting my food? Well, I didn't actually say I was counting *less* food. I accidentally ate some of the biscuits.'

GURGLE GURGLE

'You mean, they accidentally fell into your mouth!' fumed Claude. 'No wonder you have a tummy ache! How many did you eat?'

'Every last one. All 630 of them.'

'Syd!' cried Claude. 'You counted every single biscuit you ate?' Syd looked shamefaced. 'That's perfect,' cheered Claude. Syd looked confused. 'That means *we* know the place *and* the meeting time, but that DOGZ spy has got nothing!'

'Oh great,' smiled Syd. 'I told you this counting food would be useful. But let me get this straight. We're meeting our contact at Brighton Pier. But what time of day is six hundred and thirty?'

'Now you're just playing silly,' said Claude. 'It's twenty-four-hour military time. 0630 hours — 6.30 in the morning. Seems that everyone wants to get their paws on this missing piece of the puzzle. With a DOGZ spy on the loose, we're going to have to watch our backs. We've still got a while until the train reaches Brighton, and then we'll find out what's so darned important.'

Brighton Pier was England's most famous holiday destination. During the day it was a colourful tourist attraction, buzzing with the whirligig noise of carnival music. Families would be lined up under the flashing lights as they queued for fairground rides, while small kits cried over their dropped mice creams.

'What do you think?' asked Claude, as he and Syd hopped off the train.

'Mate, it's not like the beaches back home,' shivered Syd. 'It's cold and miserable and there's nobody here.'

'Well, we *have* arrived in the coldest hour of the night,' said Claude.

It was the hour before dawn and the fairground had become a dark and mysterious place. The only sound was the crash of waves against the big pillars beneath their feet.

'I don't like this,' said Claude. 'That DOGZ spy could be lurking anywhere.'

A soft wind rustled the carnival flags.

Figures moved in the dark.

The two cats sprang to attention, ready to take on any DOGZ — but it was just the fairground carousel.

Creeeeee!

The carousel gave a rusty groan as it turned in the shadows and then stopped.

Claude and Syd headed out to the very end
of Brighton Pier and found themselves a perfect
position to sit and wait for their contact.

'From here we can see the whole pier,' said
Claude. 'No one will be able to sneak up on us.'

They waited . . . and waited.

As dawn lightened the sky, a chilling fog rolled
in off the sea. The world was smothered in greyness.
Even with his superior cat eyesight, Claude strained
to see anything at all. All his cat senses were on edge.
It was 0630 hours and the two cats had no idea who
was about to surprise them.

Then suddenly . . . **PWOFF!!**

The two cats leapt in the air at the noise. It
sounded like a whale letting out a massive breath.

Below the pier, the water began to bubble
and swirl. A periscope rose from the sea,
followed by the conning tower
of a submarine. It was a very
small submarine.

Air hissed out of the valves and water poured
off the conning tower. There was a metallic
clanking as the hatch opened and out popped the
head of someone Claude recognised immediately.
There was a flash of light as the figure lit up a
catnip cigarette.

'Monsieur Claude. Monsieur Syd. You look like you've seen a ghost.' It was Yuki, a brave spy Claude had last seen in a Paris graveyard.

'I knew you were daring,' said Claude, 'but you must be totally fearless to travel underwater.'

'When the world is in danger we must do dangerous things,' said Yuki. 'I have brushed with death many times to get here.' She ran a paw past her ear and Claude noticed that a chunk was missing. 'The last time we met I gave you some plans,' said Yuki.

'How could I forget?' said Claude. 'The designs for the new Catproni plane! We've come for the missing piece.'

A commotion came from inside the submarine. '*Aiuta*! Help me, I'm being tortured in here.'

'Who have you got down there?' asked Syd.

Yuki just gave a mysterious look. She tossed Syd a mooring rope, then pounced gracefully onto the pier. From down in the submarine came a grunting and puffing, like someone escaping from a straight-jacket. Claude and Syd leaned forward as a large figure bulged out of the hatch. He wheezed and huffed before finally getting his belly clear. Yuki held out her paw. Her passenger took one large wobbly step onto the pier, where he promptly fell to his knees and kissed the wooden planks.

'Oh grazie mille, a thousand thanks. I was *dying* in there.'

Yuki helped the cat to his feet. He swayed back and forth as he got used to being on land again.

'Let me introduce . . .' said Yuki theatrically.

'. . . Valentino Catproni.'

Claude and Syd's mouths dropped open. Catproni was the most famous plane designer in the whole world.

Catproni held out his paw. 'I believe in England I should say, how you do do?'

'How *do* you do,' corrected Claude. 'From the news reports, we thought you'd been captured by the DOGZ. How did you escape?'

'Oh you-a *killing* me with this story. I was not ever captured by the DOGZ,' began Catproni. He flung his hands as if they were puppets acting out his adventures. 'No! I was on holiday, visiting Berlin, when the DOGZ army took over the old dog kingdoms. Overnight, I became a cat trapped in a dangerous city. There were DOGZ soldiers everywhere.

'For a long time I was able to hide in the shop of an antique dealer, waiting until I could escape. I knew if the DOGZ got hold of my aeroplane designs, they would rule the skies. So I made my plans into a kind of puzzle. I kept one part secret, and Yuki was able to smuggle the rest of my designs out of DOGZ territory, hidden inside a coffin.

'I am sorry to say that I am not a very brave cat.' Catproni twirled his paws dramatically. 'I was terrified that the DOGZ would capture me and torture me to build planes for them! I hear that they have a device that brushes your tail the wrong way!'

'Those mongrels!' said Syd, wincing.

'Lucky for me, Yuki *is* a very brave cat,' Catproni continued. 'Yuki was able to get me out of DOGZ territory, hidden inside an antique Persian carpet. I was rolled inside that hairy sausage for a week, without one bite of delicious food!'

'How on earth did you survive?' asked Syd.

Catproni patted his belly. 'Let us just say that I am half-a the cat I used to be. I lost so much weight

inside that rug that my suit was big enough for two —
and *that* became the secret to my great escape. Yuki and
I joined a travelling circus and disguised ourselves with
a bit of makeup. When those DOGZ came sniffing
around, they had no idea that the Siamese twins were
actually Yuki and myself.'

'We were assisted by The White Mouse,' added
Yuki. 'And my friends in The White Paw helped us
escape in this little submarine.'

'Heaven help me,' moaned Catproni. 'I never want to travel squashed, like-a sardine in a can, ever again.'

Catproni eyed Claude up and down. 'For some cats it is okay to fit inside a can. *They* are small and puny.' Catproni clenched his fist. 'But not for me! I may be a scaredy-cat, but I was born to look down from the sky when I travel.'

Claude interrupted. 'Speaking of travelling, we need to get going. Where is this secret piece of the puzzle?'

Catproni smiled and tapped his forehead. 'I keep it inside-a my brain. *That*, no one can steal from me.'

Yuki spoke up. 'As we fled in this submarine, DOGZ spies were close behind. You must protect Catproni and get him safely to London. Good luck, and au revoir.' Yuki boarded the tiny submarine and shut the hatch. Within minutes she had disappeared under the waves.

Claude and Syd escorted Catproni back along the pier, constantly alert for danger. They stumbled in the endless grey until they found the main road. At that moment, a black shape growled in the fog.

CHAPTER 5

Something dangerous stirred in the morning mist. It gave a throaty growl, like a hungry wolf. All at once, a car emerged from the grey.

It was a red and black beast with huge exhausts protruding from the bonnet like polished fangs.

It was the type of car a vampire cat might drive in a gothic storybook. The vehicle's back door flew open and out stepped . . .

. . . one of the most recognisable dogfighters in all of katdom.

'Well curl my tail and call me a poodle,' said Major Ginger Tom. 'If it isn't the famous Catproni.'

'Oh mamma mia,' cried Catproni clutching his chest. 'You nearly make-a me die!'

'It's okay, Major Tom is one of us,' said Claude, holding Catproni steady. 'Don't be afraid.'

'I'm not frightened,' laughed Catproni. 'I'm just so excited to finally meet-a the famoso Major Ginger Tom.' Catproni slapped Major Tom about the shoulders and waved his arms to Claude and Syd

as if he were delivering a speech from a high balcony.
'Oh, such a combination — the brilliant Catproni
and the daring Major Tom. It gives me shivers to
think of it.'

Claude steered Catproni away from Major Tom.
'Syd and I are taking Catproni back to London.'

'Change of plan, chums,' said Major Tom,
grabbing Catproni by the elbow.

'Allora. You're killing me,' chortled Catproni.
'No need to fight.'

'I'll take Catproni from here,' said Major Tom.
'As I said in my bestselling autobiography, "It's my

way or the highway.'"

'Fantastico,' smiled Catproni. 'All friends
we go together.'

Major Tom looked a little put out. 'Well . . .
chums . . . I wasn't planning on bringing the whole
squadron along!'

'Catproni's not moving a whisker without us,'
said Claude firmly. With that, they all piled into the
back of Major Tom's car.

Inside, heavy curtains hung on the windows
and there was a wooden panel separating them from
Major Tom's driver. Major Tom gave the panel a rap
with his knuckles and the car roared off, speeding
out of town and along the country lanes.

Claude rustled the curtains and peeped outside.
He was expecting DOGZ spies to be speeding up
behind them, but all he could see were vague shapes,
racing past in the fog. Major Tom pulled the curtains
shut. 'Let's keep our little party secret,' he smiled.
'Nice and chummy-like.'

Time seemed to stretch out forever in the endless mist. Eventually they turned down a lane where huge stone lions glared from the gateposts. The car travelled down a long driveway and Claude felt as if they were being taken into some mystical realm.

When the car came to a halt, the four cats hopped out and stood on the gravel driveway. The growling vehicle slunk off into the mist. As the fog drifted aside, they found themselves in front of an imposing mansion of orange stone.

'Welcome to Cheshire Manor,'
said Major Tom, 'my family home.'
   'It's-a charming fairy tale,' said Catproni.
   'Yeah, any secrets hiding in the tower?'
asked Syd.

'What? What tower?' said Major Tom, startled.

'The one with the great big spire,' said Syd. 'It
looks like a scene from *Kitty and the Beast*.'

'Oh *THAT* tower,' laughed Major Tom. 'That's
off limits, chums. Only the servants go up there.'
He hurried them up the stairs. 'Let's get out of
this miserable grey, shall we?'

The interior was no more comforting. They
stood in a vast hallway as two old cats came down a
cold marble staircase.

'The Earl and Lady Cheshire,' said Major Tom,
introducing his parents.

'Gingey Whinge,' glowed Lady Cheshire, pinching Major Tom on the cheek and giving it a good waggle.

'Oh mumsy,' said Major Tom. 'Not in front of the chaps!'

Major Tom's mother turned to Claude, Syd and Catproni. 'I call him Gingey Whinge because he was such a whingy little kit, always cry cry crying for his mumsy.'

'Well, luckily I had nanny to bring me up,' pouted Major Tom. 'You and father were always off on some holiday.'

Major Tom's mother took Claude and Syd's coats and hung them up. 'Gingey, your chums have arrived just in time for a wee nibble,' she said.

'I could do with a wee nibble,' grinned Syd beginning to drool.

'What about your diet?' reminded Claude.

'Yes, Syd,' said Catproni. 'You have the body of a god. You must only eat a seafood diet.'

'Too right,' said Syd. 'When I *see* food, I eat it.'
Catproni and Syd both laughed, patting their bellies.
The Earl and Lady Cheshire led them down a long
hallway with Claude and Major Tom trailing after.

They passed dozens of rooms, some with
furniture covered in white cloths, like ghosts sitting
down to dinner. The Earl strode ahead, pointing

at the paintings. It seemed like all of Major Tom's ancestors were watching their every move.

'We Gingers have been in Britain since the Bone Age,' said the Earl. 'We trace our family back to Queen Ginger the First. *Some* cats might say that *our* family are more royal than Queen Vic-Clawria herself!'

Claude was usually fascinated with history, but his mind was on the mission. He pulled Major Tom aside. 'What about Catproni?' asked Claude. 'Did Commander Snookums give you a mission briefing?'

'Briefing?' said Major Tom. 'Look chum, a cat like me doesn't have time for briefings. They're all blah blah blah and too many words. Don't you worry about the mission. *I'll* take care of Catproni.'

Major Tom wandered off with his arm wrapped around Catproni's shoulders. 'We must fly together,' he said. 'I have my own airstrip out the back, and a beaut little plane that's my pride and joy.'

'It would be like heaven to fly with Major Tom,' gushed Catproni.

'Yes, I'll send you to heaven alright,' grinned Major Tom, leading Catproni away. 'Let's head to the salon and I'll tell you about the part in my autobiography when I crash-landed in a French cream factory.'

As the others wandered on, Claude stopped at a huge window and looked out over the gardens. He was still jittery about spies, and he half expected a squad of Sniffer DOGZ to come crashing through the glass in a daring raid. But the only thing lurking in the fog were hedges cut into strange shapes. *Snap out of it*, Claude told himself. *We're in the heart of England. We're perfectly safe from the DOGZ here.*

Suddenly a terrible wail cut through the air.

'Ahhhhhhhh, you-a killing me!' came Catproni's cry.

Claude immediately flew down the corridor to Catproni's rescue.

CHAPTER 6

Claude burst into the salon ready to fight an army of spies.

'You're-a murdering my taste buds,' Catproni cried. Major Tom was pouring a glass of the Manor's finest vintage cream. Catproni took a sniff and threw up his arms. 'You English with your warm cream,' he complained. 'It is like-a bad dog breath, but-a dog

breath that comes from the heart. In Italy we let-a the cream ferment, then we chill it. You will never taste anything like it. It fizz in your mouth like you-a drinking sparkling fireworks.'

Major Tom looked quite offended, but he put on a big friendly smile and offered Claude a glass instead. Claude shook his head. It was far too early in the day to start drinking cream, and they still had to get Catproni safely to London.

'Thanks mate,' beamed Syd, taking the glass. He looked at the others. 'Well, it'd be rude to say no.' Then he downed the cream in one gulp.

'Syd, you'll give yourself a stomach ache,' warned Claude.

'Relax chums,' grinned Major Tom. 'I've got a little surprise in the next room.'

Lady Cheshire opened the doors into the dining room, and Syd's eyes practically popped out of their sockets. There were trays of steaming lobster, roasted haddock, a giant mice-cream cake and an assortment of jellies including jelly shrimp, jelly sardines and jelly minced giblets. Towering over it all was a magnificent pyramid of glasses. Major Tom's father poured a bottle of milk into the top glass and a wonderful white waterfall cascaded down into the rest of the glasses.

Claude was somehow reminded of the fairy tale
where the little kits are invited into a delicious cat-
biscuit house, only to find themselves trapped by an
evil dog. Something didn't smell right.

Above the rich aromas, Claude picked out a
distinctive odour. Suddenly, on the other side of the
table a shadowy figure appeared.

Catproni clutched his chest, and let out a scream
of horror.

The figure was brandishing a large knife!

The table had been thrown into utter chaos. Miraculously, the tower of glasses still teetered above it all. An awful silence filled the air, until Major Tom boomed with laughter. 'Claude, you're as clueless as a cask of clotted cream. Baskerville is our butler. Why, Basky's no more a dog than *I* am!'

At that moment, the tower of milk toppled over, drenching Major Tom from whisker to paw.

Major Tom lurched backwards
and went flying into a suit of
armour standing in the corner. Its
ornamental hammer thumped
down on Major Tom's head,
making his eyes twirl senselessly.

Lady Cheshire rushed to her son. 'Oh, Gingey
Whinge, can you hear me?' she wept.

Major Tom moaned aloud. 'Basky . . . dogs . . .
when I'm . . . the king . . .'

'When you're *earl*, Gingey,' corrected his mother.
'Oh he's delirious, he doesn't know what he's saying.'

Claude felt terrible. He helped the butler get to his feet.

'No use crying over spilt milk,' said Major Tom's father. 'Baskerville's been with our family since . . .' He turned to the droopy old butler. 'Since when, old Basky?'

'Since Master Tom was a kit,' replied the butler, brushing himself down. 'My mother was Master Tom's nanny.'

'One has benefits as an aristocat,' said the Earl. 'Almost every dog has been kicked out of England, but Baskerville's been able to stay on as our butler. Lucky for him, isn't that right, Basky?'

'Quite right, my lord.'

Claude relaxed a little, but then he noticed a bandage poking out from Baskerville's sleeve. The butler pulled his cuff down to hide it.

'Have you hurt your arm?' Claude asked.

'Just a scratch,' said Baskerville. 'While I was . . . training.'

'Training?' said Claude.

'Uh . . . yes . . . training the garden roses, as a matter of fact.'

'I thought you were a butler, not a gardener.'

'Chauffeur, gardener, butler – one has to do *many* little tasks,' answered Baskerville.

'You nearly kill me from too much-a surprise!' interrupted Catproni, clawing his heart.

Major Tom was still moaning on the floor. 'My mission . . . must finish . . . my plane . . . must get . . . Catproni.'

'Don't worry, Major Tom,' said Claude. 'I'll finish the mission.' He looked around for Syd. His old friend was hunched over, clutching his belly and moaning. Claude had greater worries than Syd eating too much. He turned to Catproni. 'Looks like it's just you and me,' said Claude. 'Let's get you to London, before we have any more *catastrophes*.'

CHAPTER 7

It was late afternoon by the time Claude and
Catproni trudged across the soggy fields behind
Cheshire Manor. The fog had still not cleared, but
Claude was done with waiting around. Syd followed
behind, groaning and rubbing his stomach. 'Mate, I
think I'm going to *die*,' he moaned.

'Don't *you* start being overly dramatic too!' said
Claude.

'This is like-a pain to my heart,' Catproni
was complaining. 'I not get to fly with the famoso
Major Tom.'

They clambered into their catpits and Claude

checked the dials and flicked on the magnetos. Syd swung the propeller and the engine purred into life. It was a brand-new plane, and Claude listened carefully to the grunt of *buta buta buta* as each piston fired in perfect timing. 'I saw that Major Tom has a telephone in the house,' he shouted to Syd. 'Call Commander Snookums and tell HQ that I'm on my way with Catproni. Then get yourself back to London on the train.'

Claude fumbled at his knee for the lever to check the ammunition belts. Then he remembered that this was a private plane without guns. *Thank goodness I'm not going into battle*, he thought to himself. *Especially not with a scaredy-cat like Catproni on board.*

It was dangerous to fly in the fog, but Claude could see enough of the airstrip to risk taking off. Claude pushed the throttle forward and soon he and Catproni were speeding down Major Tom's private airstrip in Major Tom's private plane. But as the wheels lifted off the grass, a bunny the size of a house appeared out of the mist.

'We're going to die!' screamed Catproni.

Claude dipped his wing. His stomach dropped.
A great green monster appeared on the opposite side.
The plane wobbled straight and Claude powered
into the air. His heart was pounding like a piston.
As they rose above the fog, Claude realised that the
creatures were just the hedges surrounding Cheshire
Manor, which had been cut into ornamental shapes.

'What-a kind-a pilot are you?!' Catproni cried
from behind.

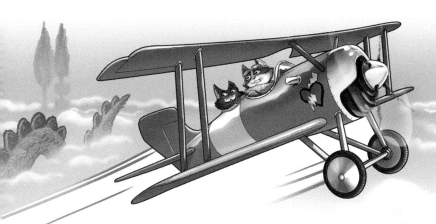

Claude ignored his precious passenger. All that
mattered was to get Catproni to CATs Eyes. As they
circled Cheshire Manor, Claude was sure he saw the
figure of Baskerville, watching from a window, then
Claude turned and headed for the safety of London.

If Claude had known what awaited, he wouldn't
have been so confident. In London, the River
Thames passed Westminster Palace and Big Ben,
then flowed under Tower Bridge. It travelled on to
the river mouth where it swept out to sea. If anyone
had been watching the river, they would have seen a
most astounding sight. First, the water rippled and
swirled. Then, the conning tower of a submarine
broke through the surface. This was no mini two-cat
contraption. This was a huge DOGZ submarine!

DOGZ SUBMARINE

1. Saw, cuts through underwater cable nets
2. Launch ramp, catapult cable and hook, helps thrust triplane into the air
3. Torpedo tube
4. Anchor
5. Bow fins, steer submarine up and down
6. Airtight chamber for aircraft
7. Conning tower with periscope and radio transmitters
8. 88mm cannon
9. Ballast tanks, air is pumped in and out of these to make the submarine rise or sink
10. Propeller drives the submarine and the rudder steers it side to side

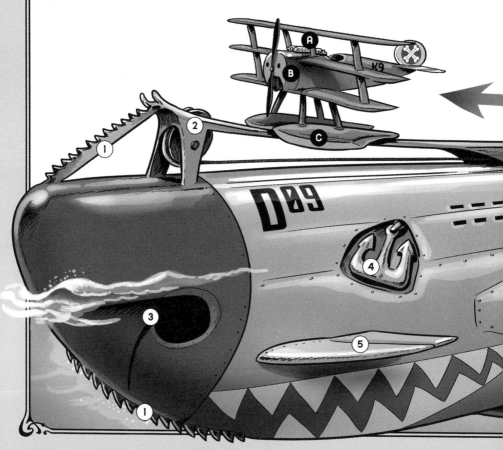

FOKKER TRIPLANE

A Two Spandau machine guns each fire 600 rounds (bullets) per minute. It was the first gun to fire synchronised with the propeller shaft, so bullets don't hit the propeller blade

B 110 horsepower Oberursel rotary engine, produces top speed of 190 km/hr

C Floats, interchangable with wheels for land use

D Wings designed to fold back alongside fuselage

There was a grinding noise. A large chamber
on the front of the submarine's conning tower
began to open up. The waterproof seals unlocked
with a powerful hiss. Inside was a red plane with
K9 painted on the side. The triplane's three wings
were specially adapted to lie back along the fuselage.
Deckhands began to fold the wings
into flying position while The
Red Setter climbed into the
cockpit. He checked the
ammunition belts, leading
to the two powerful
Spandau machine
guns, then started
the engine.

Nearby, a DOGZ navy officer
was listening to a radio transmitter, awaiting the call
from their spy at CATs HQ. The officer nodded and
gave The Red Setter the thumbs up.

'Every dog has his day,' said The Red Setter,
quoting the famous poet Shakespaw. And today was

going to be The Red Setter's day.

The propeller gave a tremendous backdraught as it wound up to full power. The deckhands held on for dear life. With a clacking bang, the catapult shot the red triplane off the end of the submarine.

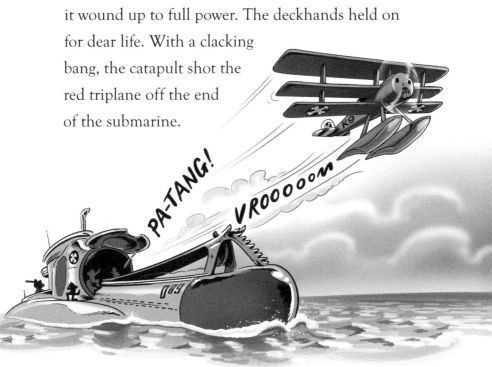

The Red Setter was airborne over England. Soon, every cat in London would know the DOGZ had arrived.

Claude and Catproni flew towards London just as the sun was setting. The sky became a dripping red watercolour over the city. On the horizon, a dozen barrage balloons floated, dotted over the tower of Big Ben and the dome of St Paw's Cathedral. *They really ruin London's famous landmarks*, thought Claude. He needed to land soon, because those blimps would be impossible to see in the dark, making it incredibly dangerous to fly.

The River Thames reflected the sky, like a pink and red pathway, guiding them in as it weaved through the heart of London. In a few minutes they'd be safely at CATs' London airbase.

Claude twisted his head to Catproni. 'We're almost there,' he yelled.

Then something caught his eye.

Behind them he saw a red glint against the dark clouds. It almost seemed like . . . no, it couldn't be — a DOGZ fighter would never have enough fuel to cross the English Channel!

But the next second he heard the distinctive chatter of a triplane's nine-cylinder rotary engine. Before he could react, the *kak kak kak* of machine-gun fire ripped through the air.

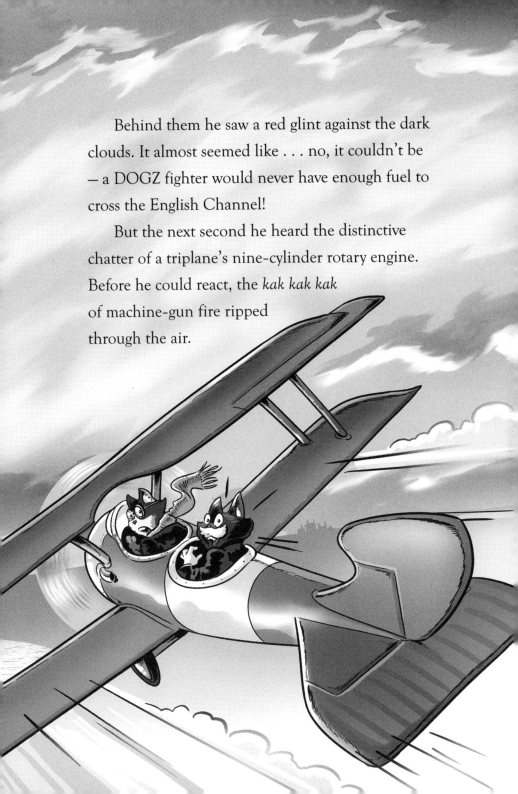

CHAPTER 8

'**A**llora!' cried Catproni. 'If only Major Tom were here!'

Claude's paw moved automatically. He reached down beside his leg to cock his machine guns. His paw grasped uselessly at the empty air, and Claude remembered with horror that Major Tom's plane had no guns!

They were an easy target silhouetted against the sky. Claude thrust the joystick forward and dived down. Moving fast over the dark rooftops, they'd be harder to hit.

The roar of engines swooped over the city streets, and Londoners were as shocked as Claude to discover a dogfight taking place above their heads. Sirens blared out across London. The sleepy old soldiers manning the searchlights fired up the generators. Soon yellow lights were sweeping the sky, like long golden chopsticks, trying to pin the planes

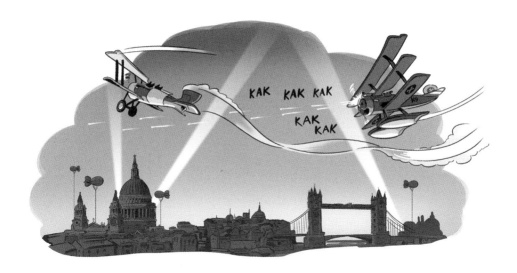

in their beams. The two aeroplanes dodged and dived between the lights like deadly mosquitos.

Claude swirled and spun, trying to outfly The Red Setter's guns.

'Woaahh, woaah, woaahhhhhhh!' wailed Catproni as they were jolted in their catpits.

This type of dogfight took an intense amount of concentration, but Claude's brain was also working overtime as he tried to dream up an escape.

He couldn't land as that required a slow, steady approach, and The Red Setter would easily blow them out of the sky. But the longer they stayed airborne, the more chances The Red Setter had to shoot them down in flames.

All the way Catproni was crying blue murder in the back catpit.

'Stop being dramatic!' yelled Claude. Then a burst of machine-gun fire tore through their engine.

'Flying furballs!' swore Claude through gritted teeth.

'We're going to die!' screamed Catproni.

'*Now* you can be dramatic,' agreed Claude.

They swooped low over the River Thames, with smoke pouring from the front of the plane.

The next attack from The Red Setter would be the end of them.

Then up ahead, Claude spied one of London's great landmarks. Suddenly he had a plan, as cunning and heroic as anything from Major Tom's autobiography.

Baron von Wolfred smiled to himself. With his distinctive red triplane, the baron had become the DOGZ' top fighter ace, earning him the name The Red Setter. The baron was extremely fond of dancing, but he also loved the graceful moves of the dogfight, and

Claude D'Bonair was certainly putting on a grand performance.

The CATs plane was hard to target against the reflections on the river. The Red Setter followed low, looking for a clear shot.

Tower Bridge was speeding towards them, and suddenly the CATs plane shot upwards. The Red Setter let go a burst of fire as it rose against the sky. The CATs plane powered on in a full loop-de-loop around Tower Bridge's upper walkway.

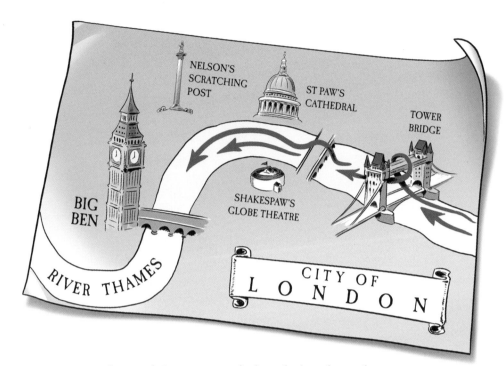

The Red Setter stayed close behind, ready
for another shot, but the CATs plane spun in a
spectacular corkscrew. It weaved through the masts
of boats moored on the river.

They raced further upstream, past St Paw's
Cathedral, then banked sharply as the river
curved left.

Since the DOGZ spy had failed to capture
Catproni, The Red Setter was the DOGZ' last
resort. If the DOGZ couldn't have Catproni, then
nobody would. It was an added bonus that Claude

D'Bonair was caught up in it all. Every cat and dog had heard of the heroic dogfighter, Major Ginger Tom, but it was Claude D'Bonair whom Baron von Wolfred admired the most. They had duelled many times. *It was almost a shame to end the dance*, The Red Setter thought to himself. But orders were orders, and his orders were to stop Catproni making it to London at any cost. The Red Setter recalled a line from Shakespaw — today he would eliminate two of DOGZ' most wanted foes 'in one fell swoop'. The Red Setter cocked his guns for the final strike.

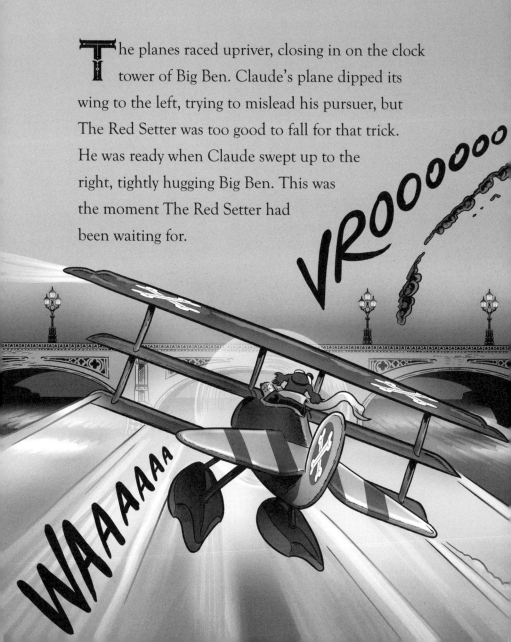

CHAPTER 9

The planes raced upriver, closing in on the clock tower of Big Ben. Claude's plane dipped its wing to the left, trying to mislead his pursuer, but The Red Setter was too good to fall for that trick. He was ready when Claude swept up to the right, tightly hugging Big Ben. This was the moment The Red Setter had been waiting for.

The CATs plane was framed in the searchlights. The Red Setter let loose a volley of bullets which tore through the CATs engine. He swept around Big Ben in pursuit, and was momentarily blinded by a searchlight beam.

There was a slicing screech. The Red Setter looked back in surprise to see his wings spinning away into the darkness. They'd been slashed off by a metal cable! The Red Setter was flung sideways as his triplane twirled in a crazy spin, before slamming to a halt. He was trapped in a cable net, dangling high above the city.

Claude glanced back. His plan had worked!

BADANG!!

Claude had led The Red Setter
straight into the two barrage balloons
floating behind Big Ben. The cable nets
were almost invisible in the dark.

But Claude wasn't safe yet. Major Tom's plane was on its last gasp. Claude listened carefully to the engine. The timing was all off, and the cylinders were firing in uneven bursts. The aircraft was like a wet dog, shaking from nose to tail.

Luckily CATs' London airbase was right in the heart of the city. As Major Tom's plane spluttered and coughed its way across the sky, the airstrip lights came on, leading Claude in to land.

With the engine shot to pieces, Claude had no power to make a controlled descent. They thumped the turf hard, ploughing a great gash in the earth for hundreds of metres along the airstrip.

As the ground crew came speeding to meet them, Claude shook his head clear. *Surely another of my nine lives gone.*

He checked on his famous passenger.

'You're-a killing me, you crazy cat!' exclaimed Catproni, gripping his heart. 'That was the most exciting ride I ever take.' He patted Claude on the shoulder. 'You-a one great pilot my friend!'

Mission accomplished, sighed Claude. He'd brought Catproni to London in one piece, but he couldn't say the same for Major Tom's beloved plane. Claude gave a groan. 'I think Major Tom's going to kill me.'

MARGRITTE'S CATNIP
EST. 1898 BELGIUM
Cesi n'est pas une pipe

the Scratching

THURSDAY EVENING EDITION

Double Cross Dogfight

CATs' highest medal for bravery, the double cross, was awarded to a heroic pilot by Her Royal Hairness Princess Kitty at Buckingham Palace today. Our reporter, Fifi Hackles, uncovers the truth behind the daring duel over London.

Cats throughout the city were shocked to discover an air battle taking place above their heads last night. Major Tom's plane was seen in a fearsome fight with the DOGZ' top fighter ace, The Red Setter. With brilliant skill The Red Setter was defeated, and Valentino Catproni was delivered to safety.

At an awards ceremony today, trumpets blared as the star of last night's dogfight showed off his glittering double cross to the public. However, those gathered were suprised to learn that the hero of the moment was *not* their favourite cat, Major Tom, but a totally unknown young pilot from CATs HQ in Paris. It turns out that this pint-sized pussycat had been flying Major Tom's personal aeroplane. Many are now saying that Major Tom deserves his share of the double cross too.

Valentino Catproni's fighter planes will soon rule the
The famous aeroplane designer will

Post

EDITOR IN CHIEF D. MURRAY. PUBLISHED BY CHAPMAN & CO. SINCE 1822

EVERYONE'S HERO MAJOR GINGER TOM

RED MENACE BEHIND BARS

Cats across the world will sleep better tonight knowing that the DOGZ' most feared fighter ace is behind bars. The infamous Red Setter has been taken to CATs' top-security prison.

MORE ON PAGE 7

AN UNKNOWN YOUNG PILOT FROM CATS HQ RECEIVED THE DOUBLE CROSS MEDAL, PICTURED BELOW AT THE CEREMONY WITH A FRIEND

WHERE'S MAJOR TOM?

While celebrations went on, one question was on everyone's lips: 'Where is CATs' most dashing dogfighter?' Rumours abound that Major Tom is sick as a dog, but most cats agree that the heroic ginger pilot must be on some daring secret mission. Whatever Major Tom is up to, it's sure to be a totally surprising reveal in his next autobiography.

DOGZ SPY STILL ON THE LOOSE

Commander Snookums from CATs HQ says t DOGZ spy is probably right under our noses.

Far from the sparkling celebrations, across the
English countryside, in the topmost tower of
Cheshire Manor, Baskerville, the dogged old butler,
was making his way upstairs. On a tray, he balanced
a glass of full cream and a plate of dog biscuits for
supper.

Baskerville looked around suspiciously before
entering the room at the top of the tower. Plans
and maps were pinned across every wall. By the
window was a small desk with a long-distance radio
transmitter, connected to the large aerial jutting out
of the roof.

'Basky, you blundering bloodhound!' blurted Major Tom. He gripped his throbbing head, which was wrapped in bandages. 'I've told you a million times not to come into my private room when I've got important business to attend to.'

'As you wish, Master Tom,' said Baskerville, leaving the cookies and cream. He backed out of the room and shuffled down the stairs again. Baskerville had known Major Tom since he was a kit, but the old butler would have been totally surprised if he had known just *who* his master was talking to on the long-distance radio transmitter.

Major Tom waited until the butler's footsteps faded before he spoke into the microphone.

'My Furrer, Alf Alpha,' said Major Tom, to the leader of the DOGZ army. 'Let's be chummy about all this. It's not my fault that Catproni got away. The White Paw are to blame. They helped Catproni escape DOGZ territory in the first place.'

Major Tom stroked his chin as he admired his reflection in the dark window. 'If The Red Setter was as good a pilot as me, he wouldn't be in prison right now and Catproni would be dog tucker!'

There was a burst of mad barking from the other end of the line. Major Tom winced and held the headphones away from his ear. 'Well pluck my whiskers and call me a pussycat. I *did* do dangerous things! I *was* brave!' he answered. '*I* was the one who broke into their train cabin.' He rubbed the bandages where Claude had scratched his arm as he'd escaped on the roof of the train.

'*I* brought Catproni to Cheshire Manor. *I* tried to poison that irritating Italian,' Major Tom growled.

'If only that blubberball Syd Fishus hadn't guzzled all the cream. There was enough poison to kill a whole battalion. Syd's got guts alright — he must have the stomach of a walrus to survive with just a tummy ache!'

There was another stream of barking down the line. 'I can understand why you would want to do that to my short and curlies,' said Major Tom. 'But steady on Alf Alpha, *I'm* not the one to blame. Claude D'Bonair is the real thorn in our side.'

Major Tom glowered. His eyes became tiny specks of burning ember. 'I vow to you My Furrer, that Claude D'Bonair's nine lives are going to run out *very* soon. But first, I've got a plan to deal with those rebel dogs, The White Paw. CATs won't last long without their dog friends.

'Remember, Alf Alpha, we have a deal! And when DOGZ win the war, I'll get *everything* you promised me! Then all those cats will find out why I've double-crossed them.'

Claude hadn't known just how right he was when he joked that Major Tom wanted to kill him.

Lamplight flickered in the high gothic tower of Cheshire Manor. It was a moment which deserved a storybook flash of thunderous lightning. But outside, it was just a quiet English night.

As Major Tom schemed and plotted, even the moon seemed to have a secret Cheshire grin.

When Donovan Bixley was seven his mother read him *The Lord of the Rings* and the following year he decided to write a sequel. This was Donovan's first book and it was called *The Return of the Balrog*. It was only three pages long.

Since then Donovan has illustrated over 100 books published in 31 countries. He has won many awards including the Mallinson Rendel Illustrators Award from the NZ Arts Foundation, and his part-comic — part-novel *Monkey Boy* was selected by the International Youth Library as one of the top 200 children's books in the world.

Find out more about Donovan and his work at www.donovanbixley.com